Meet Molly's baby sister

Mom took a deep breath. "Lucky didn't take very well to being a mother. In fact, she didn't take to it at all."

"That's really sad." I didn't know what to say. Poor little ape, I thought. "Zoey is going to live, Mom, isn't she?" I could feel my heart racing.

"Of course," Mom reassured me. "It's just that a baby orangutan needs twenty-four-hour-a-day care and love, just like a human baby. And I have to give it to her now."

I could feel my eyes narrowing. "Does that mean you have to live at the zoo?" I blurted. "You're my mom. I need you too."

Mom hugged me. "Of course I'm not going to live at the zoo. As a matter of fact . . ."

Just then we heard Brad yelling all the way from upstairs. "Hey! What's this thing doing in the bathtub?"

Mom jumped to her feet. "As a matter of fact, Zoey is going to be living here," she blurted. And with that said, she ran out of the room, and my life changed forever.

Zoey
& Me

There's an
Orangutan
in My Bathtub

Zoey & Me

There's an Orangutan in My Bathtub

Mallory Tarcher

Troll

To my partner in life and love, Brad Hood

Chapter

1

I cornered my mother on the landing, blocking the stairs so she couldn't sneak past me.

"But it's not fair," I wailed, holding up the torn shreds of what had been my social studies project and flapping them at my mom. "Look what she did! Aren't you at least going to punish her?" I was furious. All my hard work, ripped to pieces.

My mother frowned . . . at me, believe it or not, as she cuddled little Zoey in her arms. "You, young lady," she scolded, "are being very silly. Zoey is just a baby. She doesn't know any better," Mom said, stroking Zoey's red hair as she rocked her back and forth in her arms.

My mouth dropped open. I had spent the last two weeks coloring in a giant map of South America and pasting different plastic fruits on their country of origin (that means where they came from), and somehow Mom was blaming me for the fact that Zoey had torn it up. I can tell you that if I had done something like that to one of my brother Brad's projects, I sure wouldn't be getting a hug right now.

"You know to keep your bedroom door closed,

Molly," my mother continued, playing with Zoey's little hands and never taking her eyes off the baby's face.

"It was closed!" I nearly stamped my foot I was so mad. "I closed it this morning. I'm not stupid."

Then I did stamp my foot because I remembered that this project was twenty-five percent of my grade for the quarter. And it was due tomorrow. And half of the fruit was chewed up and somehow stuck to my bedroom ceiling.

"Are you sure you closed your door?" Mom asked as she made goofy faces at Zoey.

"Yes!" I said, just this side of a yell.

"Really?" Mom finally stopped playing with the baby and looked at me.

"YES!" That time I did yell, and I stamped my foot at the same time. I was really mad.

"Oh, that's wonderful!" Mom hugged me with her free arm. Then she leaned out over the stair railing and shouted for my dad. "Charles, guess what?" she yelled at the top of her lungs, just like I get into trouble for doing. "Zoey can open doors now. Isn't that fabulous? I really think she's just the brightest little girl," Mom finished.

""That's just great. Bring her down," my dad called out over the babble of the evening news.

"In a sec," Mom shouted back. Then she turned to me. "Molly, I'm really sorry about your project." She put a hand on my shoulder and looked thoughtfully at me. "Brad has a baseball game later. How about if after dinner, your father and I help you make a new project?"

"Will you put Zoey in her cage?" I mumbled as I gazed at the polished wood floor. Somehow Mom's being nice had turned my mad into sad, and I had this weird closed-up feeling in my throat.

"Of course," she said.

"Okay." I looked up at her. I could tell she couldn't wait to get downstairs and celebrate Zoey's new trick with Dad. "I'm going to see if I can get the plastic bananas out of the light socket," I said, snuffling as I turned away.

My mom went even paler than normal. (All the girls in our family have red hair and really pale skin, so it was kind of scary to watch.) "The light socket?" She looked horrified. "We have got to finish baby-proofing this house," she muttered as she headed down to join my dad.

"Be careful, honey," she called over her shoulder to me. I turned around and looked up just in time to see her back turn the corner, and to see Zoey stick out her long black-spotted tongue in my direction.

I stuck mine out at her, but it just wasn't the same. I have the tongue of a normal eleven-year-old girl. Zoey's is much more impressive. After all, she's an orangutan!

Chapter 2

I guess I'd better begin at the beginning. My name is Molly Miles, and I'm eleven years old. I have curly auburn hair (even though my brother calls me "Red") and twelve horrid freckles on my nose. And I just stopped biting my nails.

My dad is really nice. He's kind of average height and wears glasses, which are always slipping down on his nose. He is a pediatrician, and most of my friends have him as their doctor. My mom is a different kind of doctor. She is a primatologist at the Los Angeles Zoo. She knows everything about certain kinds of apes, which is why we have Zoey—but I'm getting ahead of myself.

My fourteen-year-old brother, Brad, is a sports nut. He plays baseball and basketball and is convinced he's going to make millions playing professionally someday. He wears glasses like my dad, but his don't slip as much! And although he sometimes acts like an ape, I guess he's okay.

And I have this small problem. Her name is Zoey. She's a year-old orangutan, and—as weird as this may sound—she lives with my family. Usually orangutans live with their families, but something happened with Zoey's mom, Lucky.

We had all been waiting for Lucky to have her baby. My best friend Tyler, who lives next door, had been camping out at our house for a week because Mom said we could go with her to see Lucky give birth. My dad was on call at the hospital the night Lucky went into labor, so Mom woke up Brad and me and Tyler and told us to get dressed.

It was pretty exciting. We got dressed really fast in the dark, and I ended up with one red tennis shoe and one hot pink one. Then we all piled into our light blue minivan. Seconds after we had each claimed a window seat and buckled our seat belts, Mom headed at top speed to the zoo.

The streets were nearly deserted. There is something about being out so late that's totally awesome. I don't know whether it was the hour or what, but Brad, Tyler, and I didn't say a single word as we sped through the empty streets. (And I'm not known for keeping my mouth shut no matter what time it is.)

Anyhow, we got to the zoo, and the guard waved our car through the main gates, past the public parking lot, and right into the zoo itself. It was really cool hearing the different sounds of the African jungle, the rain forest, and the savanna all in one place. All the animals were screeching, screaming, or howling to each other.

Mom barely slowed down as we drove past the elephant area and around the lion enclosure. She pulled up to the primate section, which was all lit up. She jumped out of the car and started running toward the back entrance to the infirmary, which is kind of like the nurse's office at school. She was halfway to the door before she realized we weren't following her. It's not that we didn't want to, it's just that in her excitement she had leaped out of the car, slammed her door—and locked us in! That should have been my first clue that things were about to get weird, but I was still kind of sleepy so I didn't pick up on it. I just thought it was funny.

Mom aimed her key remote at the van, unlocking it from twenty feet away. She didn't even look back as she flung open the doors to the infirmary and disappeared inside.

"Come on, kids, hurry," my brother said as he unbuckled his seat belt.

I looked at Tyler. "Kids?" I asked. "Gee, there must be an adult around I'm not seeing, huh, Tyler?" I added sarcastically. I hate it when Brad acts like he is so much more mature than I am. He's just a kid, too.

"Knock it off," Brad said, pushing past us to the van door, managing to plant one of his huge feet on mine on the way out. "You two can stay here if you want, but I'm going inside." He jumped down and headed toward the building.

Ty shrugged. "I don't want to sit in the car all night," he said.

I looked at Tyler and tried not to laugh. He had gotten dressed in such a hurry that he had pulled his sweatshirt on inside out and backward, so the little tag was sticking out under his chin.

I guess some girls would think that Tyler is cute. He has thick blond hair and blue eyes, and he's the third tallest boy in our grade. It's not that I don't think he's cute. But he's just Tyler to me, the same Tyler I used to play with in the sandbox when we were five, and got bathed with when we were three. Our mothers even took turns changing our diapers. We've lived next door to each other for so long that we've got keys to each other's house.

"I want to go inside, too." I hated to admit Brad was right about anything, but I hated missing what was going on inside even more.

Mom met us at the entrance to the delivery room. She was wearing a blue hospital gown, a silly cap, and one of those paper masks you see doctors wear on TV. Her red hair was sticking out from under the cap, and it made her look kind of like a deranged clown.

"You three come in here," she said, putting her hand on my shoulder as she half led, half pushed us into her office and away from the infirmary itself.

"But I want to see what's going on with Lucky," I whined. "You promised—"

"Nope. Sorry," she interrupted. "Lucky is having a hard time. She's scared. It's her first baby, and because she was raised in a zoo, she's never seen another orangutan give birth. In the wild, she would have seen lots of births, and she'd know what to expect." Mom kept looking back and forth between us and the delivery room. I could tell she really needed to get back to

Lucky. "You three will have to wait in here. I'll be back soon," she added.

"But—" This time Brad tried. He wasn't exactly into hanging out in an empty office in the middle of the night with his kid sister and her friend. But he didn't get any further than I had.

"Bye." Mom blew us a kiss, slipped her mask back on her face, and closed the office door behind her.

"But—" Tyler said to the closed door.

"Too late," I moaned. I knew just how he felt.

"Great." Brad flopped down on the only comfortable chair in the room. He picked up the snowman paperweight I had gotten for Mom on a trip to my grandparents' in Northern California last winter and started tossing it up in the air and catching it. Up in the air, catch. Up, catch. Up, catch. Up . . .

I took a deep breath. Brad played catch with everything. "Stop it!" I tried to grab the paperweight from him, but he just laughed, holding it high above my head, out of my reach.

And so began a really long night. I don't remember falling asleep, but I must have, because I woke up with my head on a dictionary and my arms wrapped around one of the legs of Mom's desk. Someone, I can't believe it was Brad so it had to have been Ty, took pity on me and covered me with a blanket. It smelled a little funny, but most things do in the Ape House. Phew!

I knew it was morning from the little beams of sunlight that blinked through the slats of the window blinds. I struggled to stand up straight, a difficult thing to do after spending the night sleeping in a pretzel position. I was trying to stretch all the kinks out of my shoulders when the office door opened.

"Rise and shine," Mom chanted as she entered the room. She looked far more cheerful than she had any right to, considering that she hadn't slept a wink.

"My neck hurts," I grumped. I'm known for waking up in a bad mood.

"My back hurts," Brad chimed in. He isn't "Mr. Happy" in the morning either. I think it runs in the family.

"Good morning, Mrs. Miles." Ty smiled brightly at my mom as he pushed his sandy blond hair out of his eyes. "Can I see the new baby?" he asked. "Please?"

It's funny how we're always more polite with other people's parents than with our own, I thought. I looked at Tyler and raised one eyebrow (which, by the way, is a neat trick).

"Is it a girl?" I asked.

"A boy?" Brad said at the same time.

"It's a little girl." Mom smiled at us, but there was a funny look in her eyes. She reached over and tried to smooth down my hair.

"What's wrong?" I put my hand on hers.

"Nothing," she answered. But I had the feeling she wasn't telling the truth. "Come on. I'll show you the newest addition to the Ape House. Her name is Zoey."

We followed Mom out of her office and down the hall to the viewing room. We pressed our noses against the glass wall that separated us from the nursery, searching for Lucky's baby.

I spotted her first and sucked in my breath. A little, nearly bald orange head stuck out from under a thick pink blanket, and ten really long black fingers clutched the bars of a small crib.

"Oh*hhhhh*. She's like a little doll," I whispered, fogging the glass in front of me.

"Yeah, a really funny-looking one," Brad muttered. He looked at his watch. "Mom, I've got baseball practice at nine. Our first preseason game is next week."

"Right," Mom said. "Dad will be here soon to take you guys home." She frowned, and two lines appeared between her eyebrows. "I have to stay here for a while." Mom sighed and reached up to tuck one of her curls back under the cap. In the growing light of morning, she was starting to look kind of beat.

"How come?" I asked. "Isn't Zoey okay? She looks all cozy in that crib."

Mom made a face. "That's the problem. She should be with her mother, not in a crib." She shook her head. "Lucky isn't bonding with the baby the way she should. We're hoping she'll feel better when she's rested a bit." From the look on Mom's face, I didn't think she really believed that.

Before I could ask anything else, Dad walked into the viewing room. He took a quick look at Zoey then had a hushed conversation with Mom. I tried to catch bits of what they were saying but it was no use. Mom and Dad were pros at speaking just softly enough so I couldn't possibly hear them.

After a few minutes Dad turned to the three of us.

"Let's move out, troops," he said in his do-it-now voice. "Mom has to get back to work and Brad needs to get to baseball practice."

Mom gave me a quick hug. "I'll call you later, okay?"

"Okay," I said quietly. "I hope Lucky feels better." Then I turned back to the glass wall and took one last look at the baby. "Bye, Zoey," I whispered. "Your mom will be here soon. I'll see you later." I felt kind of sorry for the little thing as we walked out to Dad's car.

Dad had brought Brad's baseball junk with him, so he dropped Brad at the practice field. Then we headed home.

"See you later, Molly," Ty called as he walked across our lawn to his house.

"Did you have fun last night?" Dad asked as he unlocked the front door.

"No. We didn't even get to see Zoey being born," I grumped. "Mom should have left us home." My head still felt like it was stuffed with cotton balls, and I don't even want to start on what my mouth tasted like after a night of breathing in ape smells.

"Well, your mother told you Lucky had some problems. And you know Mom would never leave you home alone . . ." Dad began as he settled into the couch, picked up the remote control, and turned to the sports station to catch the highlights from last night's baseball game. I threw myself down next to him, too tired to think of doing anything else.

"I'm not a baby," I whined. "And I wasn't alone. Ty and Brad were here. Not that we needed Brad," I added as I rubbed my eyes. "You guys just don't trust me." This was a running battle.

"Well, maybe next time you can stay home alone." Dad never was big on arguing. He'd usually say something soothing but noncommittal and let Mom handle the fights.

"You sure sound tired," Dad continued. He helped me off the couch and gave me a gentle nudge toward the stairs. "Maybe you should take a nap or something."

"Dad, I'm eleven, remember? I don't take naps, and I'm not tired," I muttered. I sometimes wondered if my parents fell through a time warp. They're about ten years behind the rest of us.

Boy, there is nothing like sleeping on a tile floor to leave you really cranky, I thought. I stomped up the stairs, using the banister to pull myself along, and headed right to my room, muttering, "I'm not taking a nap, I'm just going to lie down on my bed and hang out for a minute."

I stumbled into my room, glanced at my warm, soft bed, and took a flying leap. I didn't even take off my shoes—I just flopped on top of the covers, grabbed my squishy pillow, and was out like a light!

It was not a peaceful sleep. My dreams were filled with flying red monkeys. They were sort of a cross between those monkeys in *The Wizard of Oz* and the new little orange bundle in the Ape House. And they were all trying to get me.

I woke up wondering how something as cute as Zoey could have turned into something as scary as those flying monkeys. It just didn't make sense.

Mom never did come home that Saturday. Nor the next day. In fact, I didn't see her until after school on Monday.

"Hi, stranger," she cried, sweeping me up in a big hug. She looked like she hadn't slept in a week.

"Mom!" I squeezed her right back. "I've missed you!" I really had. We'd had pizza three nights in a row. It was fun the first night and okay the second, but by the third, it was really boring! Then again, it was definitely better than Dad's cooking.

"Me too, you." Mom pulled up a kitchen chair and sat down on it, patting the empty one beside her. She reached out and lifted the hair off of my face, and then tucked the strands behind my ears. She's always doing that.

"I have a surprise for you," she teased, some of the twinkle coming back into her eyes.

"What?" I love surprises. I reached up and untucked my hair from behind my ears. I like my hair in my face.

"Well, you know Zoey," she began.

"Yeah." I looked closely at Mom. She was smiling, so there couldn't be anything wrong.

Mom took a deep breath. "Lucky didn't take very well to being a mother. In fact, she didn't take to it at all. Lucky wouldn't feed Zoey, or hold her—"

"Why not?" I interrupted, horrified. "She's so cute. Don't orangutan mothers have to love their kids?" I asked.

"Well, in the wild they usually do," Mom agreed. "But as I told you, Lucky grew up in captivity, in a cage.

21

She never saw other orangutans taking care of their babies, so she never learned how to do it herself." Mom shook her head and sighed.

"That's really sad." I didn't know what to say. I couldn't imagine what it would have been like if my mother hadn't wanted me. Poor little ape, I thought. "How is Zoey going to live? She is going to, Mom, isn't she?" I could feel my heart racing.

"Of course," Mom reassured me. "It's just that, well, a baby orangutan needs twenty-four-hour-a-day care and love, just like a human baby. And," Mom paused for a deep breath, "and I have to give it to her now."

I could feel my eyes narrowing. "Does that mean you have to live at the zoo?" I didn't like the way this conversation was going. "You're my mom," I blurted. "I need you too." I had this vision of having to eat pizza every night for the rest of my life!

"Oh, honey." Mom hugged me. "Of course you do and of course I am—your mother, that is. And no, I'm not going to live at the zoo. As a matter of fact . . ."

Just then we heard Brad yelling all the way from upstairs. "Hey! What's this thing doing in the bathtub?"

"Oh, dear." Mom jumped to her feet. "As a matter of fact, Zoey is going to be living here," she blurted. And with that said, she ran out of the room, and my life changed forever.

Chapter

3

Mom and I tore up the stairs, around the corner, and into our blue-and-white-tiled bathroom. It looked like a hurricane had plowed through, leaving nothing untouched. There were towels all over the floor and bottles of shampoo and conditioner running into the sink, and I noticed this strange white chalky stuff growing on the shower curtain. Did I mention how much we all missed not having Mom around?

"Mom! Why is there an orangutan in the bathtub?" Brad looked furious. He was standing next to the tub, a towel wrapped around his waist. His scrawny legs stuck out the bottom, his hairless chest was bare above, and his fists were firmly planted on his hips.

I tried not to laugh and ended up making a half snorting, half coughing sound instead.

"Where would you have put her?" Mom asked, scooping Zoey up into her arms.

Brad wasn't quite sure what to say to that.

"Can I hold her?" I couldn't believe there was an orangutan in our bathroom.

"Of course you want to hold her," Brad muttered. "You look just like her, red hair and all!"

I stuck my tongue out at him.

He stuck his tongue out at me.

Then—and I swear I'm not making this up—Zoey stuck her tongue out at both of us!

"Sure." Mom held Zoey out to me, ignoring all the stuck-out tongues. I gingerly cupped her little orange head with one arm and held her blanket-wrapped body with the other. She felt heavy and warm.

Brad was looking back and forth between Mom and me, his mouth still open.

"By the way, nice outfit," I teased as I rocked baby Zoey.

He turned three shades of red as he looked down at himself and realized he was standing around with his mother, his little sister, and an orangutan, wearing nothing more than last year's beach towel.

"I am trying to take a shower," Brad said with as much dignity as he could muster.

"Hey, Mom, can I take her into my room?" I asked, ignoring Brad.

"All right. Just be careful," Mom answered as she bent down to pick up some towels that were shoved under the claw-footed tub.

"Would all of you please get out of the bathroom?" Brad pleaded. He looked like he was about to have a fit.

"Come on, baby," I cooed to Zoey. "I think I have some old doll clothes in my closet that will fit you."

I could see Mom smiling at me as I rocked Zoey in my arms.

"Can you send Tyler up to my room when he gets

24

here?" I asked as I headed out of the bathroom.

"Okay," Mom said, grabbing the rest of Zoey's stuff and following me down the hall.

We both heard the bathroom door slam behind us.

Sometimes older brothers just have no sense of humor!

Now, I had spent a lot of time with Mom at the zoo, so I'd had some experience with orangutans before. But Zoey was the first baby orang I had ever met.

I bunched up a big pile of pillows on the middle of my bed, including my very favorite squishy one, so that she'd be comfortable. Then I carefully laid Zoey down on the pillows, unwrapped her blanket, and just stared at her. I had propped up her red-fringed head so that she could see, and her big brown eyes never left my face.

Zoey's head and body were a pale black color, and she had spiky red hair all over her body. She wasn't exactly covered in hair—it looked more like she had been dusted with it.

At first I thought that, aside from the fur, she looked pretty much like a regular baby. Well, a regular baby with really long arms and legs and saggy skin all over her body. Her little face was all wrinkled up, and her brown button eyes had big bags underneath them. The more I thought about it, the more I realized she looked like a really tiny old lady, not a baby at all!

"Were you up too late last night?" I cooed at her.

Zoey yawned and stuck out her tongue, then closed her mouth and forgot to pull her tongue back in. It looked like a normal baby tongue, smooth and wet, except that it was covered with black blotches.

I reached out with my pointer finger and touched it. It felt like my tongue.

Then Zoey burped right on my hand, and let me tell you, I have no idea how something so small and new could make a smell that bad.

"Phew!" I jumped backward, nearly falling off the bed in the process.

Tyler, who had been standing in the doorway watching silently, started to laugh.

"Did she bite you?" he asked between chuckles.

"No." I fanned the air in front of my face. "She burped on me. Yuck. Orangutan breath."

Tyler grinned as he peered down at Zoey. "So, new baby in the house? You're in for it now, Molly."

"Huh?" I had no idea what he was talking about. "She's not a baby, she's an orangutan." Like duh!

"Is she getting lots of attention?" he asked.

"Well, yeah, but . . ." I began.

"Is she already turning the house upside down?"

"Well, not really," I said, thinking about poor Brad and looking at my messed-up bed.

"Did you fart?" he continued.

"What? No!" I protested.

Tyler sniffed the air near Zoey and laughed. "Well, then, she's got a full diaper, and that particular smell only happens when there's a baby in the house." He crossed his arms over his chest like a TV lawyer who had made his point.

"You think you know everything about babies just because you have a baby sister," I muttered. I picked up the now damp Zoey and held her out to Tyler.

"I do," he answered as he took Zoey from me and expertly swung her onto his shoulder. "But don't worry." He winked at me. "You'll learn soon enough."

Chapter 4

In the beginning it was no big deal. I mean Zoey really was just like a human baby. She slept most of the time, and when she wasn't sleeping, eating, or getting her diaper changed (yuck), she was a cute, cuddly little orange furball that loved to play. Best of all, unlike Tyler's three-month-old baby sister, Allison, whom we called "the noise machine," Zoey was quiet. She made little gruntlike noises, but none of the screaming, yelling, wake-you-up-at-three-in-the-morning sounds that human babies make.

Since Zoey was living with us, I decided to find out more about orangutans. Mom told me that orangutans are called the "people of the forest." They come from either Sumatra or Borneo and live in tropical rain forests. Orangutans are ninety-five percent exactly like humans, and it's only the five percent that's not like us that makes them look and act different.

Just like a human baby, orangutan babies depend on their parents for the first years of their lives. This is pretty unusual for animals. If you've ever had a dog, you know what I mean. By the time it's one year old a puppy is almost full grown, but even when an orangutan is fourteen years old, it is only as grown up as you and I will be when we're fourteen. And if my brother is any example of fourteen, that's not very grown up at all.

In the wild, mother orangs carry their babies all the time. It's not like they have cribs where they can put the babies down to nap, or little "tree seats" like we have car seats, so Zoey, like her wild cousins, expected to be held all the time.

The first week Zoey was with us it was no problem. Everyone in the family fought for the chance to hold our little orange baby. By the end of the first month, however, there was a lot of "Do I have to hold her, I just held her yesterday?" being shouted around the house. In fact, it didn't take long at all for Zoey to be just another red-haired member of the Miles family.

In the early days, even months, that Zoey was living with us, the only problems she caused were normal baby problems, like teething, throwing up, and throwing peas against the wall. Then, on a rainy Monday morning when Zoey was about five months old, the trouble started.

I was sitting at the kitchen table giving Zoey her bottle while Mom made my lunch. Brad was getting ready to go to a before-school basketball practice, and Tyler was due to crash through the back door any minute to walk with me to school.

Zoey liked wearing baby clothes in the beginning, but lately she had taken a fancy to ripping her clothes off and putting them on her head. Not on over her head, just on her head. Thankfully she still liked to wear her diaper, so that drizzly morning she was cuddled into my arms wearing only a Lambchop-print diaper and a yellow and pink rain bonnet. She held her bottle in one black-nailed hand, and a long red hunk of my hair was stuffed into the other.

Tyler slipped in the back door and plopped down into the seat next to me.

"Morning, Mrs. Miles," he said as he reached for a banana and began to peel it.

"Morning, Ty, want some breakfast?" Mom turned around and noticed that Tyler had already stuffed half the banana into his mouth. "Help yourself," she said with a smile.

"Mmmrrff," Ty answered, his mouth full of banana mush.

Zoey, who hadn't been the center of attention for a good thirty seconds, reached out and grabbed what was left of the fruit from Tyler's hand.

"Hey!" he protested as his breakfast disappeared. He watched dumbfounded as Zoey shoved the rest of the banana, including the peel, into her mouth. She looked up at me horrified, like it was my fault that the peel was still on it, and spit it out onto my lap.

"Mo*ooom!*" I whined. "This is gross."

"You did gross stuff when you were a baby," Mom said as she came over to the table and took Zoey from me.

"Like what?" I protested. I loved stories about when I was a baby, but I had a feeling I wasn't going to love this one.

"Well, your particular favorite was throwing up on your father," she answered.

"No wonder my allowance is so small," I muttered.

"If you'd been my kid I would have sent you back. You were such a little gross out," Brad teased as he stuck his head in the refrigerator.

"Not nearly as gross as you," I answered back. I swear, the minute Brad turned fourteen he stopped being any fun at all.

I took Zoey back from Mom. "I'll be right down, Ty. I'm just going to put Zoey back in her room and change my pants." I wiped my hand across the banana-flavored orangutan slobber that was starting to make a crust on my favorite pair of sunflower print jeans.

"Well, aren't you the little mommy," Brad teased. "Hey, you and Zoey even look alike. Red hair and all." This was Brad's favorite new insult. He said it often, and it was really beginning to bug me.

I stuck my nose in the air and left the room. Zoey screeched at Brad as we climbed the stairs. I was happy she was on my side. By the time I had gotten Zoey squared away and changed myself (twice, of course, because now I couldn't find anything I felt like wearing), Tyler was banging on the door to my room.

"What?" I opened the door and glared at him. "I'm coming!" I had been thinking about Brad saying that I looked like Zoey, and it had made me mad.

Tyler put up both hands as if to say, "Don't hit me, I'm just the messenger!"

"Sorry, come on in," I muttered.

Tyler flopped down on my chair. "So, you were in charge of our current events project. What did you come up with?" he asked, tossing his head sideways as he tried for maybe the millionth time to keep his blond hair out of his eyes.

"Oh, no." My heart started to beat kind of fast, and I got a sick feeling in my stomach.

"'Oh, no' can't mean you forgot," Tyler said, eyes wide, hair forgotten.

"Uh . . ." I was stalling for time.

"I mean you would never forget something as important as our project," he insisted. "You wouldn't, would you?"

"Of course not," I lied. I looked frantically around the room, hoping I would see something I could use for a five-minute presentation about a newsworthy topic. Every Monday, Mrs. Hurwitz, our social studies teacher, discussed current events. Two teams of two kids each had to do a presentation on some timely topic in the news. The team that had the best current events item for the week got extra credit. This week it was Tyler's and my turn, and we were up against Margie Lussman and Freddie Finkle, the meanest kids in the class.

"Well?" Tyler didn't look happy. Not that I blamed him. I had said I'd come up with something.

"Really. I didn't forget." I could feel my nose growing as I spoke.

Then I saw it. Zoey's big stuffed banana lying on my bed. "Zoey," I said with a smile.

"Zoey what?" Tyler asked.

"We're bringing Zoey." I grinned. Our project was sitting in the next room, playing with her toes.

"Right," he snorted. "We're sunk."

"Why not bring Zoey?" I stuck my chin out defiantly. Sometimes my mouth really gets me into trouble!

"Well, let's see." Tyler paused to collect his thoughts before continuing. "One, she's an endangered species." He was ticking off reasons on his fingers as he spoke. "Two, we have no way of getting her to school. Three, there's no place to keep her if we could get her to school, and besides"—Tyler sighed, pulling on his fourth finger—"there is no way in the universe that your mom will let us bring Zoey for current events. So there."

"Humph." I stalled, willing my brain to come up with answers to all of Ty's objections. "Okay, well, one, since orangutans are an endangered species, that makes them a very timely topic; two, we can take her in a big box with airholes; three, she can stay in the coat room until it's our turn; and four"—I paused here to let my brilliant plan sink in—"we'll just have to sneak her out. So there to you too!" I smiled triumphantly. I just love it when my medium-sized brain actually catches up to my extra large mouth!

Tyler grinned. "Okay. How do we get her out of the house?" he challenged.

"We leave her in her room and sneak back up the trellis on the wall near her window," I shot back.

"Fine," Tyler said, surprising me. "Let's do it." I guess he really needed the extra credit in social studies.

"Fine," I shot back. You know how you sometimes

33

start something bad and it doesn't seem possible to stop it no matter how much you want to? Well, this was one of those times. My mouth had once again landed me in major trouble, and there was no way out.

Tyler and I headed back downstairs. We found Mom in the kitchen and told her that we had put Zoey down for a nap (not exactly a lie, but very, very close).

"Bye, Mrs. Miles," Tyler said sweetly as he sauntered out the back door. "Have a nice day."

"Thanks, Ty," Mom replied. "You have a good day, too, Molly." I gave Mom a very guilty-feeling kiss good-bye and trudged out into the light rain.

Tyler and I ducked around the back of the house and worked out the rest of our plan. Zoey normally took a three-hour nap after breakfast. Mom knew we had put her to bed, so we figured that if we could do our current events presentation first, we could make some excuse about having to bring Zoey right home. We could rush home then, return Zoey to her crib, and be back at school before Mom knew any better. The plan had holes in it, but it was the best we could come up with on such short notice.

"Go on," I whispered, as the icy rain dripped down the collar of my yellow slicker and worked its way slowly down my back.

"Go on, what?" Tyler protested as he backed away from me.

"Go up and get her," I said, pointing to the window. He shook his head. "You do it."

"You're the boy."

"She's your orangutan. And this was your idea."

He had a point. I turned around and trudged to the ivy-covered wall. I pulled on the trellis, testing its strength. "Brad uses it all the time," I rationalized. And I started to climb.

One hand reach, one foot step, other hand reach, other foot shove off. Don't look down. I repeated that pattern until I was high enough to grab the windowsill outside Zoey's room.

With a heave, I pulled myself through the open window and into the room, landing in a heap on the floor next to Zoey's crib, which was a cage with lots of baby stuff in it.

Zoey looked down at me from inside her crib. She slipped her hand through the bars and patted me on the head. "Thanks," I muttered, untangling my arms from my legs.

I undid the latch to the crib, and Zoey willingly crawled into my arms. We'd been teaching Zoey to "give kisses," so I had to put up with a slobbery orangutan kiss before I could get her to hold still long enough for me to get her into her clothes.

I dressed her quickly, not forgetting her pink rain bonnet, and hurried over to the window. Tyler was standing below, looking up, rain falling into his face.

"Hurry," he whispered as he waved his arms.

Subtle, I thought. "You look like a windmill. Settle down or you'll scare Zoey," I whispered back.

Tyler put his hands down by his sides and moved back to a relatively dry spot under the tree.

I climbed down the way I had come up, but let me tell you, everything is harder with a twenty-pound orangutan hanging from your neck! I jumped the last three feet and ended up on my hands and knees in the mud. Zoey landed on top of me, riding me, "horsey" style.

Tyler had gotten an old box from the garage. There were several airholes punched in two of the sides. Zoey, who had never been a big fan of getting wet, climbed in and pulled the top flaps down without any protest. In fact, she looked cozy and warm in her new home, which was more than I could say for myself.

"Come on," Tyler said as he looked at his new Swatch. "We're going to be late."

Like that's my fault! I thought, glaring at him as I picked splinters from my fingers and brushed the mud off my pants. Okay, so maybe it was a little my fault since I'd forgotten about the project. "Fine. You carry her!" I said, walking off ahead of him.

Tyler picked up Zoey and fell in behind me for the six-block walk to school. "What are we going to say about her?" he asked as he struggled with the bulky box.

I filled Tyler in on some basic orangutan facts as we walked. I figured we wouldn't have to talk much. Once the kids saw Zoey they'd be focusing on her, not on what Tyler and I were saying. I could tell Tyler was having a hard time buying my plan, but he was having a harder time carrying Zoey. I grabbed one end of the box, and we kept moving.

We were about a block from school when we saw Freddie and Margie.

Margie Lussman was going to be fat. She wasn't exactly fat yet, but she was definitely headed there. It was the only thing I liked about her.

Margie was one of the "popular" girls. Her father and mother were stinking rich, and Margie got everything she wanted. She showed off a lot, and it seemed like her favorite thing to do was tease Tyler and me. I was pretty sure that was because she had a major crush on Tyler. I knew it killed her to see him hanging out with me.

When she spotted us struggling with the box, she grinned. I could see her small pig eyes and pointed teeth even at a distance

"Helping your girlfriend, Tyler?" she asked as sweetly as she could at the top of her lungs.

"Ignore her," I muttered.

"I've never seen anything so adorable. What do you have in that great big box, Molly?" she added smugly.

Tyler turned red from his ears to the collar of his jacket.

"It's our current events project, and it's better than yours!" I hollered back, ignoring my own advice. I have a short temper, and I seemed to start every conversation with Margie already angry.

"I doubt it." Margie had slithered across the street and was walking alongside us. "Mine cost five hundred dollars," she gloated, her squinty eyes glinting with pleasure.

Zoey, hearing a new voice, tried to stick her head out of the box. I quickly pushed the top down. "Well, ours is priceless!" I answered her. "Come on, Tyler, let's go," I said, quickening my pace.

"Well, what is it?" Margie whined as she sped up to try and see what we had in the box. She squinted into an airhole, trying desperately to catch a glimpse of what was inside.

"That's for us to know and you to find out!" I said, sticking out my tongue.

"Yeah!" Tyler agreed. And he stuck out his tongue.

"Fine!" Margie snorted. She stuck out her tongue and turned on her heel.

"Pffft." A sound came from inside the box. And there, sticking out through an airhole, was a black-spotted tongue.

Chapter 5

Tyler and I made it to homeroom just as the bell rang. Luckily, Mrs. Hurwitz was also our homeroom teacher, so we didn't have to worry about moving Zoey to another classroom. We left the box (and Zoey) with the rest of our stuff in the coatroom at the back of the class and took our seats, which were two aisles apart. Tyler and I had started the year sitting next to each other, but by the end of the first week of school, Mrs. Hurwitz had separated our desks. We weren't cheating or anything—I just had this little problem controlling my mouth. (I talked all the time.)

I tried to pretend this was an ordinary school day, but after five minutes of sitting still my legs started moving uncontrollably. I sneaked a glance at Tyler. He was sitting up straighter than usual, and he looked as if he was about to explode. I began praying silently for Mrs. Hurwitz to hurry up and start current events.

"Okay, class, all rise for the Pledge," Mrs. Hurwitz singsonged. She was one of the best teachers in the school, even though she was pretty old and she singsonged most of what she said. It was a little irritating, but we got used to it.

Mrs. Hurwitz started every day by saying the Pledge of Allegiance. At the beginning of the school year she had told us what the Pledge symbolized, and that we could each make our own decision about whether to say it or not. Some of the kids didn't say the Pledge, but I didn't mind. Today, however, I wished that Mrs. Hurwitz had forgotten about it. Time was ticking away, and I didn't know how long Zoey would sit in that box.

We all rose and, after placing our right hands over our hearts, began the familiar morning recitation.

"I pledge allegiance to the flag," twenty-six eleven year olds chanted, "of the United States of—"

CRASH! BOOM!

Tyler and I looked at each other in horror. Those noises were coming from the coatroom!

I raised my hand. "Excuse me, Mrs. Hurwitz, I think my current events project just fell over."

"Well, Molly, nothing much can happen to it now," she answered, quite reasonably.

"But . . ." I had to go and see what kind of trouble Zoey was causing this time!

"But nothing. Start again, class," Mrs. Hurwitz said firmly.

I gave a big sigh and put my hand back over my heart.

"I pledge allegiance to the flag of the United States of America," everyone intoned.

"And to the republic for which it stands." My mouth was racing through it now. "One nation . . ."

"Ms. Miles!" Mrs. Hurwitz looked mad.

The whole class turned and looked at me. I thought I heard Margie snickering.

"Are you going to a fire?" Mrs. Hurwitz continued.

"Huh? I mean, excuse me, Mrs. Hurwitz?" Going to a fire? Why do grown-ups talk so weird! I wondered.

"I asked if you were going to a fire. You seemed in such a hurry to race through the Pledge I assumed you were," Mrs. Hurwitz explained.

That time I'm sure Margie snickered.

"Oh. Uh, no, I just want to check on my, uh, project," I offered.

Just then there was another crash in the coatroom. My heart sank. She just had to let me go check.

Mrs. Hurwitz raised her eyebrows. "Hmmmm. Maybe that would be a good idea. The rest of the class will just have to struggle along without your dulcet tones."

Mrs. Hurwitz talked funny a lot of the time. It took me a minute, but I figured that she had just given me permission to go check on Zoey while everyone else pledged. That suited me fine, so I racewalked to the back of the room to see what kind of trouble my little orange ticket to extra credit had gotten herself into.

I slipped into the coatroom and shut the door behind me. "Zoey!" I whispered. Nothing. I checked in her box. She wasn't there. I checked in the lockers. No Zoey. My stomach was starting to hurt. Then, out of nowhere, someone's scarf landed on my head.

"Hey!" I blurted. It's not that my head hurt, it's just kind of weird getting hit in the face with a strip of red and green wool when you're not expecting it.

I looked in the direction of the throw. Zoey was perched on top of the coatrack. Her lips were pulled back so far that she looked like she was laughing.

"Come on, girl," I whispered. She leaped into my outstretched arms, knocking me backward a step or two.

"*Ooofff!* You're getting heavy," I muttered as I gave her a cuddle.

She replied by sticking her finger in my nose.

"Gross," I muttered, pushing her hand away.

Then she stuck the same finger that had been up my nose into her mouth.

"Yewwww!" Chills ran down my spine. "No wonder you guys still live in trees. That was disgusting, and you're not even smart enough to know it!"

I tucked Zoey back in her box, then reached into my lunch bag and pulled out a banana for her. Zoey grabbed the banana before I had a chance to peel it. "Now stay there!" I ordered as I walked toward the door. I opened the door slightly, squeezed myself out, then shut it quickly behind me. I looked up and noticed Mrs. Hurwitz eyeing me curiously.

By the time I had walked back to my seat, Margie and Freddie had started their presentation. I groaned. Now we'd have to sit through their boring report. I wondered if Zoey could be quiet for another five minutes.

I glanced at Tyler, whose eyes opened wide as if to say, "Everything okay?"

I nodded "yes" as I tuned in to what snobby Margie was saying.

"Our project is the best one that anyone is going to have all year," Margie bragged. "That's because it's the most expensive."

If my eyeballs had rolled any farther back in my head, I think they would have been stuck there.

"My dad brought it back from one of his extremely important business trips." Margie reached into a plastic bag—and pulled out a shocking pink fur coat!

I sat up in my seat and smiled. What did a fur coat have to do with current events? I wondered. Margie would never get the extra credit now.

"It's only rabbit fur," Margie continued, "but my dad says he's going to buy me a full-length mink coat in a few years, and that will be even more expensive."

Someone behind me groaned.

"That's all very nice, Margie," Mrs. Hurwitz said. She looked as bored as I felt. "But what does any of this have to do with current events?"

"Oh, yeah." Margie was stalling for time. "Well, the coat was made in Siberia, a really cold part of Russia. And Russia's been in the news a lot lately."

I looked at Freddie. I didn't like him much more than I liked Margie, but he looked really miserable up there next to her.

"This rabbit fur has been dyed," she continued in her squeaky, whiny voice. "There really aren't any bright pink rabbits." Margie's attempt at a joke was as sad as her coat. I leaned back in my chair and enjoyed the show. There was no way Tyler and I could lose today.

Suddenly, I heard an ominous creaking at the back

of the room, as if a door was opening really slowly. I was afraid to turn around. In fact, I slunk so far down in my seat that only my head stuck out above the desk.

". . . and it comes with a matching hat and muff. It gets really cold in Russia, so people need to wear all this stuff." Margie paused to put on the jacket and waited for Freddie to hand her the hat and this weird tube-shaped thing of pink fur before speaking again.

Margie had just opened her mouth to continue her bragging when a horrible sound came from right behind me. No question about it. It was Zoey, and she was screaming for me.

I closed my eyes. Maybe if I don't look at her she'll go back into the coatroom, or better yet, back home, was my foolish hope. But my luck had run out.

Zoey was not a happy little orangutan. She couldn't see me because I had slipped so far down in my chair, and she was getting angry. She screamed again, and started banging on the floor. Everyone turned around.

"Ahhh!" That scream came from Margie. "A wild animal!" She pointed at poor Zoey, who started to totally freak out!

The whole class was in an uproar. Kids were standing on their desks, shouting. Mrs. Hurwitz was singsonging, "Everything is okay, please take your seats." Margie was screaming hysterically and clutching poor Freddie by the neck, and Tyler and I were chasing Zoey around the room calling her name. Total chaos didn't begin to describe it.

And then everything went into slow motion. Margie

was still screaming, and Zoey was leaping from desk to desk. With each leap she got closer to Margie and, with each step, I got closer to Zoey. She was just inches out of my grasp when she jumped right into Margie Lussman's pink furry arms.

The two of them fell backward onto the floor, a tangle of pink and orange limbs. Only seconds behind Zoey, I couldn't stop running in time. I crashed into a heap with them. Seconds later Tyler landed on top of us.

The room grew very, very quiet. Zoey disentangled herself first and clambered in a huff onto a nearby desk. Somehow she had snatched Margie's dyed pink fur hat, which clashed something terrible with Zoey's orange fur.

And then everyone started to laugh. Even Mrs. Hurwitz was chuckling. Everyone, that is, except Margie, who started to wail.

"Aw, stop it!" Freddie hauled her to her feet. "You're not hurt. And that was the crummiest current events project ever." Margie tuned her crying down to a low moaning sound. Freddie was probably the first person who had ever put her in her place. I was going to have to rethink how I felt about him.

"No harm done," Mrs. Hurwitz singsonged.

Margie disagreed. "My hat!" She pointed at Zoey, "Give me my hat, you . . . you monkey," she yelled, reaching for the pink fur monstrosity.

Zoey had been taught not to grab things, so she reached over and slapped Margie's outstretched hand.

"Ow!" Margie got out two, maybe three whines before Mrs. Hurwitz took over.

"Stop it, Margie!" Mrs. Hurwitz could be pretty fierce. "You are not hurt, and that is not a monkey."

Margie opened her mouth to protest.

"Enough!" Mrs. Hurwitz cried, not giving Margie a chance to interrupt. "Go to the bathroom and pull yourself together," Mrs. Hurwitz added dismissively, as she held out her arms to Zoey.

I guess even Zoey knew who was in charge in the classroom. She jumped straight into Mrs. Hurwitz's waiting arms. Margie slunk out of the room, muttering angrily under her breath.

I was stunned. I hadn't figured that Mrs. Hurwitz's years of teaching experience could prepare her for this kind of assault. She got us all back to our desks and retook command of her classroom while Zoey played with one of her dangling earrings.

"Well, class," she began when we had all settled into our seats. "Look what Molly and Tyler have brought for current events."

I gulped and, for the second time on that horrible morning, slid down in my seat, hoping I wouldn't be missed.

"Molly and Tyler, would you like to come up here and tell us something about this little fellow?" Mrs. Hurwitz asked. She had this way of asking a question so that it wasn't really a question—it was more like a direct order.

I slipped out of my chair and walked up to the front of the room. Tyler shuffled along behind me.

"Um, okay." I held out my arms for Zoey. She promptly stuck her tongue out at me and buried her face in Mrs. Hurwitz's shoulder.

Clearing my throat, I tried to remember our family dinner conversations for the past ten years. "Um, Zoey is an orangutan," I began. "And an orangutan is an ape, one of the great apes, not a monkey. She is a Sumatran orangutan, from uh, Sumatra. That's in Indonesia." I smiled at Mrs. Hurwitz.

Mrs. Hurwitz nodded encouragingly. So far, so good.

"Orangutans are an endangered species," I went on. "People used to eat them, and then for a long time the mother orangutans were killed so that people could have the babies for pets. Now many zoos have captive breeding programs. This means the zookeepers plan which female orangutan gets to have a baby with which male orangutan, so that there will be plenty of them for people to see. And then maybe people will want to protect them, not kill them."

That was it. I was pretty much out of information. Boy, did I wish I had listened more at dinner!

Mrs. Hurwitz smiled at me. "Any questions, class?" she asked.

No one did anything for a minute. Then Moe Valetto, a really smart, kind of nerdy kid who always sat in the front row, raised his hand. "Can I touch her?" he asked.

"Oh, me too!" Hands shot up all around the room.

Mrs. Hurwitz agreed. She picked up her desk chair and placed it to the side of her desk. I sat down, and

Zoey, who was still wearing Margie's stupid hat, sat on my lap. One by one, the class came up to shake her hand. Zoey enjoyed all the attention and behaved like a perfect lady. Only Margie, who had finally returned from the bathroom, refused to come near Zoey.

"Well, well." Mrs. Hurwitz looked really pleased with herself. I couldn't figure out why. After all, I was the one who had brought an orangutan to first period! "We certainly have had a very educational session this week. Oh, and Margie, your coat is very nice too, I'm sure."

Margie's face went red with anger.

I looked at Tyler and grinned. "Zoey," I said loudly enough for everyone to hear. "Give Margie back her hat."

Zoey glared at me, but I knew she knew what I was saying. Slowly she plucked the pink thing off her head, buried her face in my neck, and held the hat out toward Margie.

"Come on, Margie," I said with a totally fake smile on my face. "Come and get your hat."

Margie turned an even brighter shade of red that clashed really badly with the pink coat she was still wearing. "I don't want it anymore!" she pouted.

"Oh, but it's so . . . so . . . well, I mean it does match your coat." I was trying desperately not to laugh.

"Yeach." Margie stuck her ample nose in the air. "It's got orangutan germs. She can keep it!"

I grinned. "Thank you. That's so nice of you."

I avoided looking at Tyler. There's no way I could have kept a straight face if I had caught his eye.

Before Mrs. Hurwitz could say anything else the bell rang.

We had made it! Current events was over, and as far as I could see, Tyler and I were the big winners. Someone is going to have to bring in an elephant to top this one, I gloated to myself. Now I just have to get Zoey home before Mom finds out and I'm home free!

Mrs. Hurwitz put her hands on Tyler's and my shoulders as the rest of the class trooped out of the room to go to phys. ed. I looked up at her, but she wasn't smiling anymore.

"Where is your mother, young lady?" she asked. Her twinkly eyes were no longer twinkling.

"At home," I answered. Suddenly the feeling of Zoey's arms around my neck was kind of comforting.

"And is she aware that Zoey is here with us today?"

I considered lying. "No." I opted for the truth, instead.

Mrs. Hurwitz was silent.

"We snuck her out the window," Tyler volunteered.

"I see," Mrs. Hurwitz said.

"I was in charge of our project but I forgot to do one," I offered.

"I see." Mrs. Hurwitz leaned against her desk. She was getting such a good confession out of us she didn't need to say much more than that.

"Margie always brings in good stuff," Tyler blabbed by way of an explanation. "And Zoey is a great current events project," he finished weakly.

Zoey waved her hat, as if to make the point.

"Would you like me to call your mother, Ms. Miles, or would you like to do it?" Mrs. Hurwitz was great at giving us choices that weren't really choices at all.

"She's kind of busy this morning," I began, but that sentence trailed off as soon as I heard how stupid I sounded. "I'll call," I said, making a face. Boy, is she going to be mad, I thought miserably as Tyler, Zoey, and I trudged to the principal's office.

But mad didn't even begin to cover it.

Chapter

6

Mom wouldn't even speak to me when she came to pick up Zoey. She didn't even say, "Molly, I'm so*oo* disappointed in you," which is what she usually says when I've really messed up. Nothing. Nada. Not a word.

Tyler and I were in the teacher's lounge when Mom arrived. She opened the door and held out her arms. For a heartbeat I thought they were for me. No way.

"Zoey," she said.

And the little orange traitor climbed down from the bookshelf where she was eating one of the paperbacks and ran over to her.

Mom picked Zoey up and, without a backward look, left the room.

I felt awful. I just hadn't thought about what could happen. I knew I shouldn't have taken Zoey out without permission, but I was desperate. And now Mom was so mad she wouldn't even speak to me.

As the door closed behind them, I could feel the tears building up behind my eyeballs.

"At least we beat out Margie and Freddie for the extra credit," Tyler said, trying to make me feel better.

"Yeah," I answered glumly. "But somehow that

doesn't seem so important anymore."

Ty got up from his chair. "Come on. It's almost lunchtime. Let's head for the cafeteria and be first in line. Maybe they'll even have something good today."

That made me smile. There was about as much chance of the cafeteria having something good as there was of my going home and having Mom thank me for starting Zoey's education by bringing her to school.

As it turned out, the meat mush they served us at lunch was the highlight of the day.

Tyler and I took turns carrying the big cardboard box as we walked home through the rain in silence. The bare branches that had looked clean and sleek just a few hours ago now looked dead and scary. It was the longest six blocks I'd ever walked, but all too soon I was standing in front of my house, getting ready to face the music.

"Good luck," Ty said as we parted at my driveway.

"You too," I muttered. We both knew that Mom would have called Tyler's mother, and that the odds of either of us having TV privileges for the next couple of months were pretty slim. In fact, we'd be lucky if we were allowed to do anything fun for a long while.

I shuffled up the driveway and warily poked my head inside the kitchen door. The room was empty. A burst of hopefulness swept over me. Maybe Mom forgot she was going to be mad at me and went out.

No such luck. I had one foot inside the kitchen when I heard those four dreaded words: "Molly, come in here." The good news was, it wasn't my mother who called to me. The bad news was, it was my dad, which meant I was in serious trouble. I mean, when a parent comes home from work to yell at you, you know you're in for it but good.

I pushed open the swinging door and slithered into the living room, head bent apologetically.

My folks were sitting together on the couch, looking like jury and judge all rolled into one. It looked like they had come to their verdict without hearing my side of the story.

"Sit down, young lady," my mother began.

"Mom, I—" I blurted.

"No," she interrupted, holding her hand up to stop the flow of words from my mouth. "I don't want to hear it."

"But I—" I tried again. They just had to let me explain!

"Molly Miles, I am ashamed of you." My father shook his head disbelievingly. "Your mother and I trusted you. We thought you were old enough that we didn't have to worry about you doing really stupid things anymore." He shook his head once more for dramatic effect. "I guess we were wrong."

I hate it when my dad gets that "I can't believe I have such a rotten kid" look on his face. I could feel my eyes tearing up.

"I'm sorry," I started to blubber.

"What were you thinking?" Mom asked.

"She wasn't. Thinking, that is." My father jumped in and answered her question for me.

I sniffled. It seemed the safest thing I could do at the time.

"Your father and I need your help now more than ever," Mom continued. "You know how much we count on you."

"Having Zoey here is not easy for any of us," Dad continued without missing a beat.

"You knew better than to sneak her out of the house." Mom shook her head. "Why did you do it?"

I opened my mouth, but nothing came out. I was trying to think of something that didn't sound stupid, even to me.

"Never mind. There's no acceptable excuse for endangering her like that," Mom continued.

"But I needed her," I interrupted, deciding to go with the truth. "That awful Margie Lussman always brings something cool for current events. I forgot it was Tyler's and my turn today. I didn't have anything, so I decided to bring Zoey. And Tyler and I won—we got the extra credit."

My parents were dumbfounded. They looked back and forth from me to each other as if I were speaking some language they didn't understand. I couldn't figure out why. It had all made perfect sense at the time.

"You brought an endangered species to school because you forgot to do your current events project. Is that all you have to say?" My father's voice was getting dangerously loud.

I nodded. Now that I heard Dad say it, I had to admit it sounded kind of lame.

"Molly, Zoey's safety is extremely important. Your father and I thought you knew that." Mom's forehead was all bunched up, and I could tell she was struggling to keep her temper under control.

Dad sighed. "Molly, go to your room. Your mother and I need to talk about this privately."

I probably should have left right then, but all of a sudden I got mad. Really mad. This never would have happened if Zoey hadn't moved in, I thought. And then I exploded.

"Zoey this, Zoey that. It's all I hear these days. Suddenly your precious Zoey is more important than I am. And I think it stinks! I wish that stupid orange ape would go away so that we could be a normal family again. No more diapers, no more bananas. I hate bananas, and I'm tired of Brad saying I look like Zoey just because I have red hair too!" I knew I wasn't making a whole lot of sense, but all the bad feelings I'd been keeping inside just came pouring out of my mouth, like someone had left the water on and a flood had been let loose.

"I wish Zoey would go back to the zoo. Then maybe you'd still love me . . . not that stupid orangutan." And with that, I burst into tears and ran up the stairs two at a time to my room.

Chapter

7

I flung myself face-first down on my bed and cried into my pillow. About halfway through a good self-pity session I heard a knock on my window. I looked up, and there was Tyler's slightly panicked face. I guess he had good reason for looking scared—he was twenty feet off the ground.

The same trellis that runs up the wall in front of Zoey's window is in front of mine, but Ty and I had never used it as a ladder before today.

I hopped off my bed, ran to the window, and opened it.

"You don't like the stairs, anymore?" I asked as I grabbed Tyler by the sleeves and hauled him over the windowsill, nearly undressing him as he crashed to the floor.

"Mrrfff!" was his muffled reply.

I flopped down on the floor and waited for him to find his way back into his sweatshirt.

"Hey!" he grumped as his head emerged from the stretched-out neck hole and he sat down beside me. "You don't have to be so rough."

Tyler and I leaned back against the window seat and

rested our heads on its cushion. The nice thing about having a best friend is that you don't always have to talk to communicate. I knew he was feeling lousy, and he could probably sense from my red eyes and sad face that I wasn't in a great mood, either.

It was about four in the afternoon. The rain that had started as a morning sprinkle had grown into a late-afternoon storm, the first really big one of the season. The thickening clouds blocked what was left of the weak autumn sun, and a light mist from the rain was blowing in the open window and onto our faces.

"So, how much trouble are you in?" I finally asked as I glumly wiped the tear tracks off my cheeks.

"No TV for a month," he moaned. "And I got the 'You're our big kid not our baby, so we expect more from you' speech. How about you?"

"Well, I got the slightly more unusual 'You're our big kid not our orangutan speech,' but it amounted to the same thing," I complained. "And they haven't told me what my punishment is yet."

"Oh, that's bad," Ty sympathized.

I nodded my head. "I bet they're trying to think up something really terrible to do to me." My imagination was out of control. I wondered for a moment if there was a law preventing parents from making their kids' lives totally miserable. Then I realized there probably wasn't, considering that adults make all the laws. I was doomed.

I turned around and looked out the window. The

storm had blown off whatever leaves had been left on the trees. The branches were bare now, and there was a soggy brown mass of wet leaves on the ground below. "It looks as depressing outside as I feel inside," I muttered.

There was a knock on my bedroom door.

Ty and I looked at each other, eyes wide.

"Hide!" I whispered.

No one had ever told me that Ty shouldn't climb up the trellis, but it was one of those things I just knew wouldn't go over well with the parents. Especially since I was awaiting sentencing.

"Coming. Just a sec," I shouted for the benefit of the mystery person behind door number one.

Ty and I frantically looked around my room for somewhere to stash a five-foot-tall, ninety-five-pound boy.

"Under there." I gestured at my quilt-covered bed.

Ty dove for cover and—whack!—his head hit the drawers my dad had installed under the bed frame the weekend before.

"Sorry!" I whispered. I clamped my hand down on his mouth to stop the scream of pain I just knew was trying to get out from behind his teeth. "I forgot!"

The person behind my door knocked again, harder this time.

"Just a sec!" I half hollered. "I'm getting dressed." I hauled Ty to his feet and glanced anxiously around my room. "The closet!" I hissed to Tyler.

We both lunged for the closet door at the same time,

managing to get in each other's way twice before I stepped back. Ty leaped into the closet, pausing only to glare at me through the unkempt maze of shirts and summer dresses before closing the closet door in my face.

I took a deep breath and opened the door to my room.

"Brad?" I squeaked. He never came to my room. I realized with a sick feeling that I must be in bigger trouble than I thought.

"Can I come in?" he asked.

"What? Oh. Sure." I stepped back, and he walked past me into my bedroom. I poked my head out around the door and took a quick, spylike look up and down the hallway. All clear, I thought to myself, before hopping back into my room and closing the door.

Brad had made himself comfortable on my window seat and was watching me, a half smile playing on his face.

I stood by my bed, arms crossed over my chest. "What do you want?" It had been years since my brother had come to see me in my room, and I had a feeling he was up to something. If he wasn't on a spying mission for Mom and Dad, then he had obviously come here to tease me about my stunt with Zoey. What a creep.

"Are you okay?" Brad asked seriously.

My jaw dropped in amazement. The last thing I expected Brad to be was nice.

"Why?" I wasn't sure that he was being sincere, so I kept my distance.

Brad frowned. "I'm just asking if you're all right. I'm not the one in trouble."

I sank down onto my bed. "I know," I said miserably. "I am."

Brad leaned back against the window. I held my breath, hoping he wouldn't notice that it had somehow mysteriously gotten wet on the inside.

"This Zoey thing has been kind of tough on you, hasn't it?" Brad suggested.

"Don't say her name!" I covered my ears, trying to block out the offending sound.

Brad laughed. Not a mean laugh, more like an understanding one. Now I was really confused.

"What?"

Brad leaned forward. "You may not believe this, but I used to feel the same way about you."

"Thanks," I muttered. Now this was the Brad I'd grown not to like.

"No, wait. Imagine how I felt when you came along," Brad insisted. "I was a perfectly happy three year old, an only child, the center of attention. Then you came home from the hospital," he said accusingly.

"Well, that's not my fault," I protested. "It's not like being born was my idea."

"Well, duh." Brad made a goofy face. "But you were all cute and pink and new, and everyone spent all their time playing with you and ignoring me."

"I was cute?"

Brad rolled his eyes. "I thought you were okay," he conceded. "But then everyone made such a fuss about 'the baby' that I got really mad at you. Mom even caught me throwing toys at you one day while you were trapped in your playpen."

I wasn't sure what to say. Lately, my comments to Brad were limited to "go away" and "I'm telling." This kind of conversation was a whole new thing for us.

Brad shrugged. "I guess what I'm trying to say is that you're having to get used to a new baby in the house just like I did. Only no one is giving you credit for that because Zoey is an orangutan. At least when I was having trouble getting used to you, people understood that it was just sibling rivalry."

I was dumbfounded. Here was Brad, who never understood anything anymore, being the only person who really did understand. My head was starting to hurt from trying to figure it out.

"Thanks." This time I said it like I meant it. "I'm glad you understand."

"Yeah, well, you know, you do have to get over it," he added.

"But it's not fair," I protested. "I liked being the baby." I was surprised to hear myself say that.

"No kidding," Brad commented. "You could get away with anything. Whenever we had a fight, Mom and Dad automatically thought it was my fault because I was older."

"Is that why you hate me?" I asked.

"What? I don't hate you." Brad looked genuinely shocked that I had said that.

"Well, you sure act like you do," I countered. "I

mean you never want to hang out anymore. You never want me to do stuff with you, and you tease me all the time. You must hate me."

"I don't hate you!" he insisted. "It's just that . . . well, you're my kid sister. There's a big difference between fourteen and eleven."

"Almost twelve," I interrupted.

"Almost twelve, then," he conceded as he stood up and walked over to me. "It would look weird if I hung out with you. But I don't hate you. I love you, even if you do look like Zoey," he said, tugging on my red hair to make his point.

"Wow." I was stunned. "You know, you're okay, too." I couldn't believe that popped out of my mouth, but then, it had been a strange afternoon all around.

"Thanks." Brad looked as surprised as I was. He got up from the window seat and walked over to the door. "If you want to talk or anything . . ." he offered.

"Sure," I answered.

Brad banged on the closet. "See ya, Ty!" Then he grinned at me and left, closing the door quietly behind him.

I stood staring at the closed door. Ty! I remembered in a panic. I rushed over and let him out of the closet.

"You are a pig," Ty muttered slowly as he picked his way through last year's winter clothes and this year's summer dresses, and past my new school outfits. "Don't you ever throw anything away?" he asked, stepping over several pairs of worn-out tennis shoes and out into the room.

"Sorry." I was still freaked out from my talk with Brad, so I couldn't even offer Ty an explanation for my messy habits.

"I've got to go," Ty said, starting for the door.

"No way." I pointed at the window. "Out the way you came in. I'm in enough trouble without having to explain to my parents why you're saying good-bye before you ever said hello."

Ty shrugged, and without a backward glance, he climbed through the window and was gone.

Before I could talk myself out of it, I headed down to the living room . . . and my parents. Just apologize, I said to myself as I descended the stairs. They love you. They'll forgive you. They . . . "Are gone!" I finished the sentence out loud. The living room was deserted.

"Mom? Where are you?" I shouted from the bottom of the stairs.

"Don't shout in the house," she yelled from the kitchen, answering my question without knowing it. I walked slowly through the living room, then stopped suddenly.

"Hi," I whispered, poking my head in around the swinging door that led to the kitchen.

"Hi," Mom answered. She was standing at the sink washing lettuce for our salad.

"Need some help?" I offered.

"Sure." She handed me a wet bundle of leaves. "Dry these." Mom turned her attention to the meat loaf.

"Mom?" I still was being a little tentative. "Can I ask you a question?"

"You just did." She grinned at me. "But you can ask another."

I wasn't feeling good enough to joke yet, but I smiled back at her anyhow.

"Was I cute when I was little?" I didn't look up from my lettuce-drying.

"You still are." She didn't look up either.

"No*oooo* way. Now Zoey's cute." I was feeling a little weepy as I said that.

Mom put down the ground meat she'd been pounding and wiped her hands on a paper towel.

"Zoey is a very cute orangutan. You are a very cute girl—in fact, you're my beautiful, very favorite, never-to-be-replaced girl." She enfolded me in a hug.

I stayed there for a long minute, happy to be in her comforting arms, wishing for a second I could be little again. Then I pulled back.

"That was pretty dumb bringing Zoey to school," I admitted.

"Yup, it was right up there," she agreed.

"I mean she might have gotten hurt or something." Then I smiled.

"What? What's funny?" Mom asked.

"You should have seen Margie's face when she saw Zoey wearing her hat!" I tried to hold back the laugh. I wasn't sure whether Mom was ready to laugh with me yet.

"Mrs. Hurwitz told me." Mom was grinning now. "Isn't Margie that unpleasant girl who has a crush on Tyler?"

I nodded. "Don't ever let him hear you say that. I mentioned it once and he nearly bit my head off."

Mom and I started to giggle.

"I don't want you to think I approve of what you did." Mom got the words out between laughs.

"No, I know," I spluttered. Suddenly I was feeling much better.

"It's just that I do understand. You see, there was this awful girl named Gina that I went to elementary school with . . ." Mom began.

"Honey, I—oh. Sorry, am I interrupting something?" Dad came over and put his arm around Mom's waist.

"No." Mom winked at me. "Just girl talk."

I figured it was now or never. "I'm really, really sorry," I blurted.

Then silence. I figured this was when they would tell me what horrible punishment they were going to give me. No television? Was I grounded for life, doomed to spend eternity with the dust balls that mutated under my bed? Was I—

"We know you are, honey. It's okay." Dad broke into my fantasies.

"Let's just drop it and move on," Mom suggested.

"No punishment?" I squeaked in surprise.

"Do you want one?" Dad asked.

"No!"

"Well, okay then. Would you please go tell your brother that it's his turn to set the table and to take out the garbage. Go on, get!"

I got. But this time, instead of yelling for him from the bottom of the stairs like I usually do, I went to his door and knocked. I figured it was time I started acting more grown-up.

Chapter

8

Now, I don't want you to think that after that heartwarming talk with my family everything suddenly got perfect. It didn't. Actually, it wasn't long after our chat that I discovered Zoey eating my social studies project. I think the plastic bananas got her attention, and then she couldn't stop herself from eating the rest of the plastic fruit and the poster board.

True to their word, Mom and Dad did help me make another map. They even gave me some good ideas for new things to add, and by the time we were finished my new map looked ten times better than my old one ever had. Even Mrs. Hurwitz was impressed—she gave me a B+, but she suggested I do my next project by myself. Do teachers have some sort of built-in radar?

Overall, things got a little better with Zoey. Maybe I was getting used to not being the baby in the family, or maybe Mom and Dad were more sensitive to my feelings. Maybe as Zoey got older she got to be more okay, more of the time. Any way I looked at it, having an orangutan as a little sister wasn't the hardship it had started out to be. I have to admit it even started to be fun—except when Mom and I took Zoey shopping with us.

Just before Christmas Mom and I decided to go to the mall. We live about two miles from the best mall ever built. It used to be the Beverly Pony Park when I was little, but they tore that down a few years ago and built a huge shopping paradise.

Mom and I had been planning this final pre-Christmas shopping trip for two weeks. We had picked a day that Dad had off from the hospital. He had promised he would stay home and take care of Zoey so we would be able to shop till we dropped. But when your dad's a doctor, you learn that sometimes promises have to be broken.

We almost made it out the door. Mom had her "mad money" stashed in one of her boots in her closet. ("Mad money" is money that mothers save to take their daughters shopping . . . at least that's what it is in my family.) She was just digging it out of her boot when Dad's beeper went off.

He got up to call in to the hospital, and I buried my face in my hands. "Oh, no," I moaned.

I jumped up from the couch where Dad and I had been hanging out only seconds earlier. "Come on, Mom, hurry," I shouted up the stairs.

"What's the rush?" Mom asked as she tromped down the stairs to join us in the living room.

"Nothing, let's go." I didn't want to still be home when Dad got off the phone. Then he'd have to stay home and we could have our day out as planned.

"The rush is, your daughter heard my beeper go off and she knows what that means," Dad said as he hung up the phone. He reached over and ruffled my hair.

"Don't," I found myself whining.

Remember how I told you that my dad is the doctor most of my friends go to? Well, some of my worst enemies do too. And guess which enemy (I really have only one) got sick on the day of the great shopping marathon?

"Bad news?" Mom asked.

"Appendicitis," Dad answered.

"Oh, you have to go then?" Mom asked.

"Maybe it's just gas?" I offered hopefully.

"No such luck. It's one of the girls in your class, Molly. Margie something," Dad said as he raced to the hall closet and reached for his coat.

"Lussman?" I couldn't believe it.

"Yes. You know her, don't you?" Sometimes fathers just don't have a clue.

"I hate her," I muttered.

"Really?" he asked as he searched his jacket pockets for his car keys and wallet. The worst part was, he looked surprised.

"Since kindergarten," Mom added on my behalf. "Don't you pay attention, dear?"

My father chose not to answer that question.

"Sorry." He held up his hands. "I've got to go. The emergency room doctor is afraid the appendix might rupture if we don't remove it immediately."

"But what about Zoey?" I wailed. "Mom and I were going to go shopping. We can't take her with us."

"Sorry, honey." Dad gave us each a quick kiss in the

hallway. "I'll try and be home in a few hours." And with that, he was gone.

I stood there staring at the front door. "I hate her!" I nearly stamped my foot.

"Me too," Mom agreed.

"You do?" I couldn't believe my mother was saying that. I didn't think she hated anyone.

"Sure. I don't like anyone who's mean to you. I don't hold her responsible for this afternoon, however," she added reasonably.

"I do," I muttered as I stomped over to the couch. "Boy, don't I just!" I wasn't feeling even the slightest bit reasonable. I knew Margie was probably going to show off her scar the minute she came back to school. And I was sure she'd get mountains of expensive presents from her parents because she was in the hospital. Some kids have all the luck.

"Molly, come on. We'll take Zoey with us," Mom offered.

"No way."

"Why not?" Mom asked. "She's a girl, too. Don't you think she'd enjoy shopping?"

I put both my hands on my mother's cheeks and leaned in close to her face. "Zoey is an orangutan," I said, speaking slowly and clearly. "She is not a girl. She's an ape."

"Well, she's a girl ape," Mom said matter-of-factly.

"I give up." I flung myself onto the couch.

"Look, either the three of us go to the Beverly Center, or the three of us stay home. Your choice." I think Mom was tired of my attitude.

"Fine," I groused. "Then let's go. But it's not going to be the same."

"You may be surprised. It just might be fun," Mom said, trying that old positive-attitude thing.

Just getting Zoey dressed took fifteen minutes. We tried lots of outfits on her, but she kept pulling them off for some unknown reason. I finally sat Zoey down in front of the growing pile of clothes on the floor and told her to pick out an outfit. She chose teal blue corduroy pants, a lime green sweatshirt, and bright orange socks. I put the clothes on her, and she squealed with delight at her reflection. The fashion police might arrest us in the mall, but at least Zoey was happy.

With that battle over, we faced our next challenge: getting Zoey buckled into the car seat. This task becomes much harder when the "bucklee" can undo the seat belt with her hands and her feet! Mom finally managed to get the harness buckled and gave Zoey a stern warning to leave it alone. Personally, I was exhausted by the time we pulled out of the driveway.

We found a great parking spot in the underground garage at the Beverly Center. But getting Zoey out of the car and into the covered stroller turned into yet another test of wills.

"If this is what having a kid is like, I'm never going to have one," I muttered, as I narrowly stopped Zoey from slamming the car door on her own fingers.

"If you don't want to have one, that's fine," Mom responded, as she pried Zoey's toes off the stroller harness. "But really, most babies aren't nearly this tough."

With Zoey finally strapped into her stroller, we locked the car and headed to the elevator.

"Please don't let there be anyone in the elevator," I prayed silently. "Please, please, please."

The elevator door opened, revealing two old ladies. I shook my head. "This just isn't my day," I muttered.

No sooner had the door closed and the elevator started upward than we heard a low moan coming from the stroller.

I started to cough to cover the sound, but the moan got louder.

"Aw, the baby's upset," one of the old ladies clucked.

"Poor little baby must be scared of the elevator," the other agreed.

Mom and I looked at each other over the stroller and rolled our eyes.

Hurry, elevator, I silently urged. Mom looked like she was doing the same.

Then Zoey started to rock back and forth. The stroller picked up the rhythm, and, still inside, Zoey started to laugh her demented high-pitched laugh.

I looked at the wall and tried to pretend I was someplace, anyplace else.

The minute the elevator doors opened, the two old ladies ran like they were being chased by monsters. Not that I blamed them, although I was surprised they could move so quickly. In fact, I would have joined them if Mom hadn't been holding on to the back of my jacket.

Needless to say, we cut our shopping trip pretty short. Mom got a few last-minute gifts, so she was happy. Since I was pushing the stroller, I spent most of the time trying to make sure no one I knew saw me, and I ended up with nothing. Dad and I went shopping later that week for our last-minute bits and pieces. He let me help him pick out Mom's present—a new briefcase with her initials engraved on a metal plate that was shaped like an orangutan. I bought Zoey a new stuffed banana for Christmas.

The holidays flew by. Christmas Day seemed almost surreal. What I remember most was Zoey sitting in a huge pile of wrapping paper, carefully placing ribbons on her head. She seemed to think the paper and ribbons were her presents. She played in the pile of discarded wrappings for hours, choosing ribbons to put on our heads. Everyone except Brad thought this was cute.

Christmas dinner was interesting, too, especially after Zoey decided to smear sweet potatoes all over her chest. When she started spooning cranberry sauce on top of her head, I lost my appetite.

Tyler and his family went to his grandparents' house in New Orleans for the holidays, so I spent my vacation watching movies, playing with Zoey, and helping Dad clean the garage. All in all, it wasn't a bad week.

But all good things come to an end. When Tyler and I walked into homeroom on Monday, Margie Lussman was back, and she spent the entire morning regaling the class with stories about her appendix. She even promised that she'd bring her preserved appendix in for her next current events project. The other kids turned and looked accusingly at me. They all knew Dad was Margie's doctor. I made a mental note to tell Mom to divorce him. Luckily for Dad, he left town on Wednesday for a four-day conference.

I nearly jumped for joy when Friday finally arrived. I was glad to have the weekend "Margie-less," and I was looking forward to watching Star Wars movies, eating popcorn, and hanging out at home with Tyler. Mom and Zoey were going to be home too, but they didn't really count, if you know what I mean.

Luke had just met Obi Wan Kanobi when the phone rang. And rang.

"Please grab that," Mom shouted from the top of the stairs. "I've got my hands full."

Translation: I'm busy with Zoey. But I grabbed the phone anyhow.

"Hello?"

"Is this the Miles residence?" the voice asked.

"Put it on pause!" I whispered to Tyler as I threw him the remote control.

"What?" the voice sounded puzzled.

"Not you, sorry. What was the question?"

Tyler was having trouble figuring out the remote.

"Is this the Miles residence?" the voice repeated.

"Yes." Then, to Tyler: "Give it here, I'll do it."

"Hello, excuse me." The voice was sounding kind of cranky at this point. "Is your mother home?"

"She's busy. Who's this?" I asked.

"Coach Winslow," the voice answered.

"Brad's already at basketball practice," I said, for no reason in particular.

"I know. Young lady, I need your mother now!" The voice was beyond cranky.

"Mom," I hollered, not bothering to cover the mouthpiece of the phone. "Coach Winslow needs you!"

"Is something wrong?" Mom shouted back.

"Is something—oops, sorry, is something wrong?" I had shouted the first half directly into the mouthpiece.

"Yes," Coach answered after a suitable pause. "Your brother has broken his leg and is being taken to Mount Cedar Hospital. Tell your mom to meet us there." He hung up.

I took the stairs two at a time.

"MomBradbrokehisleg." I poured the sentence out without pausing between words.

"What?"

"Coach said Brad broke his leg. He's being taken to Mount Cedar Hospital and you should meet them there."

Mom took a deep breath. "Okay, grab your things and we'll go."

"But Mom, Tyler and I don't want to go. We want to stay home and watch *Star Wars*."

"Out of the question. I'm not leaving you home alone at night."

"I'm not alone, Tyler's here."

"This is not the time for this discussion, young lady. You're coming with me, and nothing you say is going to change my mind." Mom was busy grabbing her purse.

"Zoey. What about Zoey?" I blurted. Then I grinned. Game. Set. Match. I knew I had her this time.

Mom stopped cold. I could see her brain running through all the options, but she either had to leave Zoey alone, or leave me home with Tyler and Zoey. There was no way she was going to bring Zoey to the hospital with her.

"Okay. Okay. I'm sure you'll be fine," she assured herself.

"Yahoo!" I screamed. It probably wasn't the most sensitive thing I've ever said, but it sure felt good.

"Don't 'yahoo' me. Your brother is in the hospital," my mother said as she raced into her bedroom to collect her purse and jacket.

"Sorry." I sort of meant it.

Mom quickly put Zoey to bed, and after giving us tons of instructions about what to do, what not to do, and what to be careful doing, she left.

"Whew!" I looked at Tyler and grinned. "Can you believe it—we're home, we're alone, Zoey's safely tucked into bed, and we have ice cream in the freezer!"

"Yahoo!" Tyler cheered.

Great minds think alike.

Chapter

9

Despite what you might think, chocolate-fudge ice cream and popcorn are a terrific combination. We made it through a ton of both during the first movie in the Star Wars trilogy.

"More?" I grunted, waving the next videotape box around.

"No, I'm stuffed." Tyler still had his head in the giant popcorn bag and was routing around for any popped corn hiding among the greasy duds at the bottom.

"More movie?" I asked, making myself clear this time.

"Yeah. Okay, sure."

I got up to put in the new movie and realized I had to go to the bathroom. I cued up the tape and headed for the stairs. "I'll be right back," I shouted over my shoulder. "Don't start the movie yet."

I took the steps one at a time (an hour and a half of eating junk food slows me down). By the time I got to the top of the stairs, I really had to go. I reached the bathroom door and turned the knob, but for some reason the door was sticking. It felt like a wet towel had fallen off the hook behind the door and had somehow gotten wedged under the door.

I pushed harder. It felt like a whole set of towels had gotten wedged. I gave the door one final shove and it grudgingly slid open. I stepped into the bathroom and peered around the door to see what had fallen. But it wasn't a what. It was—

"Zoey!" I shouted, quickly followed by, "Tyler, get up here!"

I dropped to my knees and cradled Zoey's little orange head in my lap. She was drooling, but this wasn't the time to worry about some orangutan slobber on my jeans.

Tyler was there in a flash. "What's wrong? Oh, my gosh!" He got the picture quickly. "What happened?"

"I don't know. She's breathing, but she threw up over there." I pointed to a spot right near the tub. "And there," I pointed to a spot near the toilet. "And—"

"Look." Tyler grabbed a plastic shampoo bottle that had fallen to the floor. The lid was off. Tyler held it upside down. It was empty.

Just then Zoey burped a bubble. It smelled like Vidal Sassoon shampoo. An improvement over her normal smell, but not really a positive thing.

I was starting to get scared. Mom had trusted me to look after Zoey while she was gone. Boy, you sure blew that one, didn't you, I scolded myself. Before I could sink further into the quicksand of self-pity, I leaped to my feet. It was time for some action.

"We have to call 911," I urged Tyler. "Can you carry Zoey downstairs?"

"Sure." Tyler reached down and picked her up. Her

limp little body leaned heavily against his chest.

"Come on." I dashed down the stairs to the phone, leaving Tyler to struggle with Zoey.

I dialed 911, and the phone at the other end rang once before a woman's voice came over the line.

"Hello, Emergency, how can we help you?"

"My name is Molly Miles. I live at 6521 Columbus Avenue. My parents are out for the evening, and our orangutan swallowed a whole bottle of shampoo."

Silence.

"Hello?" I asked.

"Young lady, we have a trace on this call. Your parents will be notified that you are making 'phonies' to the emergency 911 line. Good-bye."

"Wait!" I shouted at the dial tone. I slammed down the receiver and turned to Tyler. "Let's go get your parents."

He shook his head no. "They went out to dinner," he answered.

"Then we'll just have to take Zoey to the hospital ourselves." My heart was beating really fast. Zoey was turning green, which is a particularly bad color if you're supposed to be orange.

"How can we do that? We don't drive, and even if we did, we don't have a car." Tyler was being logical, and it was making me mad.

"We'll have to take our bikes. I'll put her in my big front basket."

"Do you remember the last time we took her out of the house without permission?" Tyler cautioned.

"This is different," I reasoned. "I have to get her to the hospital. Mom's there, and she'll fix everything."

Tyler shrugged. "Okay. But we'd better hurry. She looks like she's going to be sick again."

I grabbed the small throw blanket off the couch. "No time to get her dressed," I muttered. "Let's go."

We grabbed our jackets and reflective vests from the kitchen, then ran to the side of the house where our bikes were parked.

I gently arranged Zoey in the basket and put my old helmet on her head. Tyler and I had our own helmets buckled in record time, and once our reflective vests were pulled on over our jackets, we headed out into the night.

I pedaled slowly down my block, trying to get used to the feel of the bike with thirty pounds of orangutan over the front wheel. Tyler circled nervously around me. No doubt about it, it was going to be a long ride.

"Are you okay?" he asked. "Do you want me to take her?"

"No, I'm fine." I started to pedal harder and found that the weight was easier to maneuver the faster I went.

"Okay," I shouted to Tyler, who had fallen a bit behind. "I've got the hang of this. Let's go."

Zoey burped her appreciation.

We made a left turn at the bottom of our street and headed out onto Victory Lane. I pedaled faster, feeling the strain in my legs.

Tyler pulled up alongside me. "Are you okay?" he asked.

I nodded, then remembered it was nighttime so he couldn't see my head bobbing up and down. "Fine," I grunted. "I sure hope we don't get in trouble for this," I added.

"I'm with you on that one. The last time we took Zoey out of the house without permission, I missed four new episodes of *Star Trek Voyager*," he complained.

"Gee, and I didn't get punished at all." I grinned at him, even though he couldn't see me.

"I can see your teeth flashing, and that's not funny."

I closed my lips. "Which way on Magnolia?" I asked.

"Left."

We pulled up to the light at Magnolia. Dad always says that if you are riding your bike in the street, it is much safer to ride in the middle of the lane so the cars can see you.

We moved into the left-hand turning lane. I couldn't use my left hand to signal with Zoey in my basket, so Tyler signaled for me. Luckily, traffic was light.

Getting the bike going again once I'd stopped was a lot harder than I thought it would be. I guess it's a momentum thing, but after a scary few first seconds where the front wheel was wobbling uncontrollably, we were underway again.

By now we were at least a couple of miles from my house. I had broken about sixteen different rules and would probably be grounded until I was twenty-four, but Zoey was whimpering loudly, and I just didn't care. I had to get her to the hospital.

As we made the last turn onto Cold Water Canyon, a

really big street that even Brad wasn't supposed to ride on by himself, I saw the red emergency light flashing at the hospital. Less than a quarter mile to go.

We pulled into the emergency entrance right behind an ambulance. All the hospital staff was busy dealing with the guy inside, so they didn't really pay much attention to two kids on bikes.

Tyler dropped his bike and rushed over to help me with Zoey. He held my handlebars steady while I got off and wrestled Zoey up, over, and onto my shoulder. Then Tyler carefully wrapped the blanket around her so she was completely covered.

"Ugh." I could feel my legs start to buckle. Between the late-night bike ride and lifting Zoey, I was beginning to realize that I wasn't in great shape.

"Do you want me to come in?" Tyler asked.

"Yeah, if you want to."

"Are you sure you've got her? She looks heavy." Tyler must have seen me stagger as I hoisted her out of the basket and onto my shoulders.

"No, I'm okay. I've got to get her inside. Can you deal with the bikes?" I asked as I walked toward the emergency entrance.

"No, I'll just leave them here to be run over. Don't worry about it," he muttered sarcastically as he tried to push them both at once.

I heard a crash as one of the bikes fell over. "Ouch!" Ty moaned as I slipped through the automatic glass doors.

It took a while for my eyes to adjust to the glaring

lights inside the emergency room. I stood against a wall just inside the door and blinked, trying to catch my breath. I had hoped that somehow, magically, Mom would be waiting for me and I could turn the whole problem over to her, but no such luck. I was on my own, and Zoey's life was in the balance.

There were people everywhere, some crying, one guy screaming, and doctors and nurses rushing from one person to the next. I hugged Zoey tighter and heard her sigh in my ear. She wasn't even squirming. Not even raising her head enough to look around. Nothing.

I have to get some help or she'll die was the only thought that kept racing through my mind.

"Out of the way, kid." A paramedic pushing a gurney rushed past me.

I waited for him to pass and made my way through the throngs of people to the desk. "Don't worry, Zoey," I whispered in her ear. "I'm going to get you some help. Don't worry." I think I was reassuring myself more than her.

There was a nurse talking on the phone behind the desk. She didn't look up when I rang the little bell that advertised "Ring for service."

"Uh, excuse me," I said.

No response. The nurse kept right on chatting.

"Hey!" I shouted.

That got her attention. Sort of. She looked as if I had just interrupted the most important conversation in the world. "May I help you?" she barked. She didn't sound like she meant it.

I took a deep breath. "My, uh . . . sister swallowed a bottle of shampoo. I think she's really sick."

"Insurance?" the nurse asked in a bored tone of voice.

"What?"

"Please fill out these insurance forms." She shoved a giant stack of papers toward me, then abruptly turned her attention back to the phone call.

I squinted to read the name on her badge.

"Uh, Dana," I interrupted.

She looked up angrily but didn't say anything.

"My father is Dr. Miles," I began, "and . . ."

Well, let me tell you something. Anyone who says that there's nothing in a name is dead wrong. Dana jumped up like someone had set her seat on fire. (Thank goodness.)

"Well, why didn't you say so?" she asked, just the way the Wizard of Oz asked Dorothy that when she told him the Good Witch had sent her.

I didn't think there was much point in answering that question so I just blurted, "I need a doctor. Now!"

Dana shouted someone's name, and before I knew it, there were two people in surgical scrubs asking me questions, most of which I couldn't really answer.

One of the orderlies tried to take Zoey from me. "I've got her. She doesn't like strangers," I protested. "I'll carry her." I knew that if they found out Zoey was an orangutan before I could get her into one of the examination rooms, there was no way they would treat her. Of course, there was no real guarantee that the

84

doctors would even help her then, but at least I'd stand a chance.

I kept looking around, but I didn't see any sign of Mom.

"How old is your sister?" the nurse asked.

"She's about nine months old." I was starting to feel shaky now that there was someone else to take the responsibility from me, or at least to share it with me.

"She's big," someone commented. The doctors and nurses could only see the blanket I had draped over Zoey to keep her warm, but I guess she was larger than your average toddler.

"Please help me," I begged. "My mother left me in charge and I really messed up." With that, I started to cry. Quickly we were hustled into one of the little examination cubicles.

"I know your dad," said a lady whose name tag read Dr. Campbell. "Isn't he out of town?" she asked.

I nodded and sniffled.

She reached for Zoey's blanket. I knew I couldn't hide the fact that she was an orangutan much longer, so I let her pull it back to see the patient.

The room, which had been noisy, filled with people shouting orders, suddenly fell quiet.

"We don't treat animals here," one of the nurses said disdainfully, shaking her head in disbelief.

Well, let me tell you, I was the one who couldn't believe it. The nerve of that nurse! "She's not just an animal, she's an endangered animal," I exploded. "And she's a member of my family." As I said it, I realized that was true. Zoey was my little sister, ape or not!

"My mother left me in charge," I continued, "and if you don't help Zoey she's going to die. And it will be all your fault, because I got her here as fast as I could!" I was practically shouting.

"Take it easy," Dr. Campbell soothed. "No one said we weren't going to help her," she added, glaring at the nurse. "Now you," she said, pointing at me, "give me my patient and go sit in the corner so we can work."

I did as I was told.

I sat quietly, a first for me, and watched them take Zoey's blood pressure and listen to her heart. One of the orderlies came over and knelt down next to me.

"Do you have the poison?" he asked.

Wordlessly I pulled the shampoo bottle out of my jacket pocket.

"Good," he said as he patted me on the knee. "That helps a lot."

I tried to smile at him, but I couldn't. All I kept thinking about was how much fun I'd had with Zoey— the times she let me dress her up, the games we played together (her favorite was "hide the banana"), and the giggles I got seeing people's reactions when they met her for the first time.

"Where's your mom?" the orderly asked.

"I don't know," I sniffed. Then I realized that I did know. Sort of. She was in the building somewhere. Maybe this guy could help me find her. "She's here. My brother broke his leg." I grinned. I didn't mean to sound so happy about it, but it felt like the first thing that had gone right all night. "Can we find her?" I jumped up from my seat.

"Shouldn't be too hard. What's her name?"

"Dr. Maggie Miles. She's here with my brother, Brad." I was shifting excitedly from foot to foot.

"I'll go see what I can find out." He winked at me and ruffled up my hair, but for once, I didn't mind.

He slipped out of the room, and I looked back at the table to see what they were doing to Zoey. They had put a tube down her throat, and I could hear her throwing up. Again.

I closed my eyes and felt the tears start to trickle down my cheeks. Poor baby, I thought.

I walked around the doctor and nurses to the head of the bed. Zoey was strapped down. Her eyes were huge, and I could see how frightened she was. First she felt sick, then she went on a wild bike ride, and now she was strapped down to a table while a whole bunch of strangers did stuff to her that probably hurt. She didn't know that they were trying to help her, and there was no way that I could explain it to her. All I could do was reach over and take her hand.

He fingers closed around mine and squeezed. It hurt, but the tighter she held on, the less scared she looked.

Well, if she breaks my fingers, at least I'll be in a good place to get them fixed, I thought philosophically. After all, if I'd been paying more attention, this never would have happened.

Suddenly, all the commotion stopped. One of the

nurses pulled out the tube, and everyone backed away from the table.

I looked at the doctor, panicked. Had they given up? Was she going to die?

"She'll be fine now," Dr. Campbell assured me. "We'll put her on a saline drip for a while to rehydrate her, but Zoey's going to be okay."

It was amazing. Even the nurse who had said the hospital didn't treat animals cheered when Dr. Campbell made her announcement.

"Thank you," I said, and buried my face in Zoey's neck.

This time I was crying from happiness. In fact, I was going to have to share Zoey's drip and get rehydrated myself if I cried any more that night!

Chapter 10

Somehow Tyler found us in the maze of cubicles near the emergency room. He'd sneaked past the front desk and peeked in a few other cubicles before finally sticking his head in ours.

"Everything okay?" he asked as he noiselessly shut the door.

"Yeah," I began. "Thanks, Ty. I don't know what I would have done without you."

"You would have had to hide the bikes by yourself," he joked. "No big deal. I'm just glad Zoey's okay."

As soon as Zoey saw Tyler, she held her arms up for a hug.

She had a "thing" for Tyler, and as I looked at him hugging my little Zoey under the harsh fluorescent lights, I almost saw why. Tyler had always been my friend, but ever since Zoey arrived, Tyler and I had gotten even closer. He always seemed to know what I was feeling, and having him nearby made me feel better. I realized I didn't just think of him as the kid next door anymore.

Before I could confuse myself further by trying to figure it all out, there was a knock at the door.

I guess Dr. Campbell had told everyone who had

helped to keep their mouths shut about her unusual patient, because no one new came in. But each of the nurses and orderlies who had worked on Zoey came into our cubicle with a little treat for her.

Surprisingly, my favorite turned out to be the nasty nurse.

"Hi!" she whispered as she poked her head around the door.

"Hi," I answered curtly.

"I brought something for Zoey." She hesitated. "Mind if I join you three?" she asked.

I shrugged. "Suit yourself." I was still mad about her earlier comment.

She walked into the room. "My name is Carlie," she said, as if we couldn't figure that out from her name tag. "I figured if Zoey was going to be a patient here, she should look like a patient," Carlie continued.

I looked over at Zoey, who had one very long finger stuck up her nose, while her other hand played with her toes.

I raised one eyebrow. Unless they shaved her bald and did some pretty radical surgery, Zoey would never look like a regular patient.

Carlie held up a green gown. "Does she wear clothes?" she asked.

Zoey saw the gown and started to clap. (I told you she had opinions about what she wore, but I didn't say they were good!)

"Yeah, she loves them. Can we unhook her and get her dressed?" I asked.

"Sure." Carlie smiled at me. "And we've found your mother. We'll go see her once Zoey is camouflaged."

Tyler groaned. "This is the part where we get yelled at, right?" he half teased.

"Don't worry," I said with more confidence than I felt.

Carlie and I dressed up Zoey and got her into a wheelchair. She even insisted on wearing the silly green paper cap. I guess it was an adult-size cap because it fit over Zoey's entire head.

"How's my brother?" I asked, when Zoey was settled.

"He's fine," Carlie replied. "Just out of surgery. Your mom is with him now, and she knows we're on our way. Come on."

"I'm hating this," Tyler muttered as we left the room behind Carlie. "Whenever you have a brainstorm about Zoey, I get punished," he grumped.

I grabbed his hand and didn't let go. He was making me very nervous.

Zoey loved being pushed in the wheelchair, so she didn't protest as we snuck out into the hallway. I was sure someone would start pointing and shouting as soon as we left our room, but we wheeled along without a hassle. I think people in hospitals are so busy worrying about themselves or about their loved ones that they don't notice much about anyone else. It's the only reason I can think of why none of those people noticed two kids pushing an orangutan in a wheelchair!

Still, as I walked the halls on the way to find Mom and Brad, I had to admit that I was thinking more about what Mom was going to say than about what a bunch of complete strangers thought of our entourage.

"Molly!" We had turned one last corner in the labyrinth-like corridor and ran smack into Mom.

"Mom, I—" I began.

"Oh, Molly, I'm so sorry." She grabbed me and gave me the hugest, hardest, longest hug ever.

"Huh?" It was the best I could come up with. I was totally confused.

Mom moved back, held my shoulders, and gazed into my eyes. "I never should have left you in charge of Zoey. That's my responsibility, not yours. If you hadn't thought so quickly and reacted so smartly, something terrible might have happened, and it would have been all my fault." She sniffed, tears welling up in her eyes.

Mom grabbed me and hugged me again. "Thank goodness you were so smart and grown-up about the situation."

I looked at Tyler over Mom's shoulder. He shrugged as if to say, "Don't ask me, she's your mother."

"Uh, don't worry about it, Mom," I said, patting her shoulder. "It was no big deal."

Mom dropped to her knees and quickly checked Zoey. "She looks fine," Mom said, grinning. "Thank goodness."

"How's Brad?" I asked, feeling quite generous at that moment.

Mom shrugged. "Why don't we go on into his room and you can see for yourself."

The five of us—Mom, Carlie, Tyler, me, and Zoey—dutifully trooped into Brad's hospital room. When I saw him lying there, I was shocked. He looked terrible. My big brother looked like a little kid—kind of pale, hair all messed up, and scared. And let me tell you, no one looks good in a hospital gown. I think they picked such an ugly color just so people would automatically feel better when they were well enough to wear their own clothes.

"Hey!" Brad grinned at me from the hospital bed. "Trying to upstage me, huh, Red?"

"Not possible. Zoey won't wear plaster," I joked, ignoring the "Red" comment and pointing at his cast.

"Yeah, well, I'm not that fond of it myself."

"Does it hurt?" Tyler asked.

"Not too much," Brad admitted. "It did, but then the doctor gave me some pain medication."

His eyes did look a little goofy. I held up my hand and made a fist. "How many fingers am I holding up, Brad?" I teased.

Brad tried to laugh, but I guess his leg hurt when he moved it because he started to moan.

Zoey, who was bored with the wheelchair now that the novelty had worn off, scampered out of the seat and across the room. Before we could stop her, she was lying on the bed next to Brad giving him a cuddle.

"Hey, what's with her?" Brad griped as she vaulted over his broken leg.

"I don't know, Brad, but I think she wants to stay here with you tonight."

"No way," he protested. "Keep her away from my leg."

"Yes way," I joked as I headed out the door. "You know something"—and here I paused for maximum effect—"in those puke-green hospital gowns, you two sure do look alike!" Boy did it feel good to say that! "See ya." And, with a friendly wave, I closed the door to his room behind me.

Well, of course, Mom didn't let Zoey spend the night with Brad. We waited until he fell asleep, then the four of us piled ourselves and the bikes into the van and went home. I convinced Mom to let me sleep in Zoey's room. Even though everyone said she was going to be fine, I didn't want to be too far away from her.

Mom put my sleeping bag on the floor, and as I lay down, holding Zoey's little orange hand through the bars of the crib, I realized how much I loved my baby oranga-sister.

"I'm going to be the best big sister in the world," I whispered to Zoey.

As if she understood, she squeezed my hand and tried to pull me closer to her.

"You love me too, don't you?" I grinned in the dark as I propped myself up on one elbow.

Zoey squeaked her response and pulled me even closer.

"Do you want to tell me something?" I asked. I knew it couldn't be true, but I put my face up to her crib, anyhow. Maybe our bond was even stronger than I thought.

Zoey got up on one of her elbows. She put her face right against mine . . . and burped.

The smell almost knocked me over. But this time, I really didn't mind.

Zoey
& Me

WHO GAVE MY ORANGUTAN A PAINTBRUSH?
BY MALLORY TARCHER

Molly's having a bad day. Her sister, Zoey—who just happens to be an orangutan—trashed her room. Her brother teased her at breakfast. And when Molly arrives at a fundraiser for the local zoo, she has to sit next to Margie Lussman, the snobbiest girl in school.

But then things begin to look up. A famous artist buys Molly's painting and tells her she's very talented. Molly is thrilled—until she discovers that the artist has bought a picture *Zoey* painted! Should Molly reveal that he spent $500 for a Zoey original? Only one thing is certain: Life stinks when your sister is an ape.

ISBN 0-8167-4278-2

Troll